BACK
OF THE
BUS

Aaron Reynolds

ILLUSTRATED BY *Floyd Cooper*

PUFFIN BOOKS
An Imprint of Penguin Group (USA) Inc.

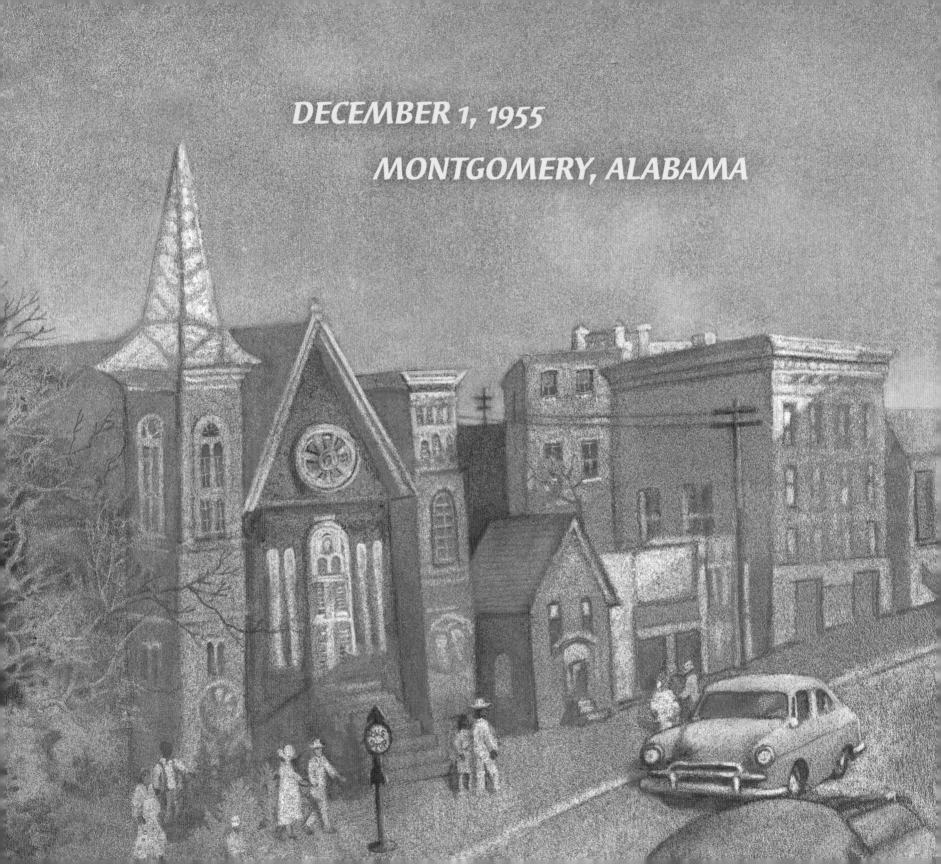

DECEMBER 1, 1955

MONTGOMERY, ALABAMA

Winter's here in Montgomery,
but I got the window down
and a warm breeze blowin' in
as Mama and me
huff down Cleveland Avenue
on the big ol' bus.

We're sittin' right where we're supposed to—
way in back.

I take out my marble,
all shiny and bright
like a big ol' tiger's eye,
and lay it on the grooves in the aisle.
The bus slows down
and that marble rolls and rolls.
But a dark hand jumps out
from a seat up front
and grabs my marble good!

But it's just Mrs. Parks from the tailor shop.
She looks back, smilin', flings a wink at me,
and sets that marble back in its groove.
That bus takes off again
and my marble comes right back to me,
like I got it on a string.

Mama shakes "no" at me,
and I hold it snug in my hand.
She's got them worked-all-day eyes,
but she's got her strong chin on.

The bus slams to a stop,
door slingin' open,
and people pilin' on,
all crammed like lima beans.
That long dark aisle's
all packed in,
jammed up tight,
and I'm glad my marble's
tucked in safe.

"Y'all gotta move, now."
It's Mr. Blake, the driver.
I can't see him
'cuz of the people jam,
but I know that growly ol' voice.

Some folks get up, new ones sit down,
  but still that bus is sittin' there stopped.
"Why ain't we goin', Mama?" I say all soft.
"Hush, child," she says.
  And I do.

Somebody's talkin' back,
but I can't hear the words.
Just Mr. Blake sayin', "I'm gonna call the police, now."

We sit and sit,
not goin' no place.
Nothin' to do but sweat,
so I roll my marble on that sticky ol' seat
and catch it before it goes down the crack.
But Mama says, "Put it away, child."
I hear Mama's crinkled-up somethin's-wrong voice,
and I hunker that brown tiger's eye down deep into my pocket,
like it's hidin'.

Some folks look back,
  givin' us angry eyes.
"We do somethin' wrong, Mama?" I say all soft.
"No, we ain't," she says.
  But I ain't sure,
  'cuz I'm gettin' shaky legs.

Same folks are doin' mean scratchy whispers
at somebody sittin' up front.
And then I see who it is
from way in back.
Mrs. Parks, that's who.
She don't belong up front like that,
and them folks all know it.
But she's sittin' right there,
her eyes all fierce like a lightnin' storm,
like maybe she does belong up there.
And I start thinkin' maybe she does too.

Fifteen whole minutes we sit,
but it feels like a big bunch more.
That breeze is long gone,
and I want me a drink real bad.
But then the policeman comes.

He walks right on my bus.
I'm all shaky inside now.
Them lima bean people spread aside,
and he stops at that way-up-front seat.

"Why won't you move and give this man your seat?"
  he says to Mrs. Parks.
  But she don't move.
  She's just sittin' in that seat
  like a turnip pile.
"I don't think I should have to stand up," she says.
"Why do you push us folks around?"
  Her voice is all soft,
  but she's got on her strong chin too, just like Mama's.

That policeman clicks them metal things on her hands,
quick and loud like the screen door slammin',
and off the bus they go.

More people sit,
and the air ain't warm no more.
She's gettin' hauled off to jail or worse,
and I'm watchin' out the window.
Mama too, with them long tired eyes.

"There you go, Rosa Parks, stirrin' up a nest of hornets,"
Mama's sayin' in her to-herself voice.
But I hear.
I see somethin' too—she's got Mrs. Parks' lightnin'-storm eyes now.

"We in trouble, Mama?" I say all soft.
"No, we ain't," she says. "Don't you worry none.
 Tomorrow all this'll be forgot."

But I got somethin' in me,
all pale and punchy,
sayin' it won't be.

Don't know why.
But instead of feelin' all shaky,
I feel a little strong.
Like Mama's chin.

I take out my marble
and start to hide it in my squeezy-tight fist.
But instead, I hold it up to the light,
right out in the open.
That thing shines all brown and golden in the sunlight,
like it's smilin', I think.
'Cuz it ain't gotta hide no more.

The illustrator wishes to acknowledge Steven Cody, Jr., the primary model for the boy in this book.

To my parents,
Paul and Barbara Reynolds,
who taught me to believe in myself
A.R.

For Virginia
F.C.

PUFFIN BOOKS
An imprint of Penguin Young Readers Group
Published by the Penguin Group
Penguin Group (USA) Inc.
375 Hudson Street
New York, New York 10014, U.S.A.

USA / Canada / UK / Ireland / Australia / New Zealand / India / South Africa / China
Penguin Books Ltd, Registered Offices: 80 Strand, London WC2R 0RL, England

For more information about the Penguin Group visit www.penguin.com

First published in the United States of America by Philomel Books,
a division of Penguin Young Readers Group, 2010
Published by Puffin Books, an imprint of Penguin Young Readers Group, 2013

Text copyright © Aaron Reynolds, 2010
Illustrations copyright © Floyd Cooper, 2010

All rights reserved. No part of this book may be reproduced, scanned, or distributed in any
printed or electronic form without permission. Please do not participate in or encourage piracy
of copyrighted materials in violation of the author's rights. Purchase only authorized editions.

THE LIBRARY OF CONGRESS HAS CATALOGED THE PHILOMEL BOOKS EDITION AS FOLLOWS:
Reynolds, Aaron, 1970– Back of the bus / Aaron Reynolds ; illustrated by Floyd Cooper. p. cm.
Summary: From the back of the bus, an African American child watches the arrest of Rosa Parks.
ISBN 978-0-399-25091-0 (hardcover)
1. Parks, Rosa, 1913–2005—Juvenile fiction. [1. Parks, Rosa, 1913–2005—Fiction.
2. Segregation in transportation—Fiction. 3. Civil rights movements—Fiction. 4. Race relations—Fiction.
5. African Americans—Fiction.] I. Cooper, Floyd, ill. II. Title. PZ7.R33213Bac 2009 [E]—dc22 2008018109

Puffin Books ISBN 978-0-14-751058-7

Manufactured in China

1 3 5 7 9 10 8 6 4 2

The publisher does not have any control over and does not assume
any responsibility for author or third-party websites or their content.

ALWAYS LEARNING

PEARSON